ARS

FVTVRA

DIDO
QUEEN OF
CARTHAGE

by

IAN CHARLES LEPINE

and

MARÍA GARCÍA ESPERÓN

ARS FVTVRA

ARS FVTVRA
Editorial Matter: Ian Charles Lepine

© 2017 Ian Charles Lepine
© 2017 María García Esperón
Cover: *Circe* by John William Waterhouse
Avenida Lomas de Plateros, edificio D4, 41
Lomas de Plateros, 01480
Mexico City
ISBN: 9781549685026

Visit: https://arsfuturapress.wordpress.com

This book is a free translation-cum-adaptation-cum-retelling of María García Esperón's novel *Dido para Eneas*. The main changes between this and the original include but are not limited to many things.

0

I know you cannot hear me, Aeneas, and that even now the oars of your ship dive into the briny waves like rays of light, and carry you away from my shores.

I know that some cruel God, being jealous of that divine happiness that is the privilege of mortals, has rubbed two destinies together and kindled forgetfulness in your heart to make you forsake Dido and her kingdom of Phoenicians and promises.

Blinded by the mightiest of the Gods, I left behind a name and a crown, broke conjugal faith with the ashes of sorrowful Sychaeus, and forgot about the future and the forces of the past. Ensconced in that joyful present, in that cave, after that failed hunting expedition, where the falling rain dispersed the men, I, Dido, Queen of Carthage, tore you away from your son, Ascanius, to carry you into the shores of my infinite love.

Of course I would like to be sorry, sorry for having driven you away from your path to Hesperia, where

Gods or voices have decreed that you will kindle a new fire, but I am not.

I am not who I was, I am not even who I am right now. And thus, I am not to blame for having become the victim of merciless Eros, of that divine daemon who made me love you above it all, for making me wish to build the kingdom of Carthage only to lay it at your feet. I am not to blame for wanting everything to bear your name, Aeneas, the Trojan, son of Anchises and Venus.

Maybe you can hear me. Maybe the winds and waves whisper my words into your ears, and perhaps even now you can feel them haunting you like a ghost, torturing you like a memory, and burning you the like the fires and Furies of remorse.

That is what I want.

I want you to suffer.

But maybe I am not myself right now. I am feverish, scared, scarred, scattered among my memories, and I have decided to die, Aeneas.

I have decided to leave this world, fighting against myself, with your sword in hand and heart, bearing it in or rather through my bosom; your sword, that glorious gift you granted to me when you accepted my love and loved me back will be my blackest ravage, but upon whom? Upon you or myself?

I have deceived everyone. My sister Anna thinks that I will conduct a ritual to burn remembrances to cinders. She thinks I will regain the life of a queen, of a founder, of a builder, a warrior, a Phoenician… But I do not wish to live. I desire neither this realm nor any other. I wish to be a slave to the shades of Hades.

I want no air or sun. I will not be married to any of those kings that were once scorned by Queen Dido of Carthage, and to whom a title-less, a Dido-less Dido must not beg for help.

I do not want to live; without you, I simply do not.

I relish not a life devoid of your grey eyes, of that sorrowful gaze with which you used to speak silent tenderness into my soul. Without you, I do not want anything but to be nothing.

I curse you, and don't want to curse you. I love you and hate to do so. I have enjoyed your gentle caresses, and now will enjoy the sharpness of your sword. I shall descend into Hades and seek Sychaeus; before him I will sink to my knees and beg forgiveness for having forgotten him. The blame was Venus' or Tanit's, he will believe that.

Even then, even though I will be a shadow, I will still continue to languish after you, and in the infernal mists I shall write your name: every day of my death I shall ask for the names that have sailed through the dreadful Stygian waters, and I shall not rest until I find yours.

Everything is now ready, Aeneas.

Order your men to row with all the strength their despair will lend them, command them to drive you away from the accursed shores of Carthage; beseech the winds for help, make sacrifices to the Gods; weep, weep like a child in Venus' lap; fight, fight like a wolf driven into a corner. Long, long for a short life and for a quick death in some forgotten swamp of Hesperia, because no one will ever as much as I did, and you shall never come across another love as mine.

You have destroyed it all by obeying the injunctions of some cruel God, of some mistaken mask of destiny, of some starved and misguided augur, of some envious divinity or man, jealous of our happiness, of everything that was, of everything that is, between the names of Dido and Aeneas.

I walk towards the pyre. I accept the sailing of your ships, your departure over the wine-coloured flood. I promise you that my hands will not tremble when in that endless moment of death, I drive your sword into my breast, where even now the wound of your betrayal drags me into the abysm of myself.

I promise you that I will die joyfully, even though I will die of sorrow, immolating myself with your double-edged love.

Forever, Aeneas.

I wonder... What if in the zenith of the pyre, when the flames seem to scorch the very heavens, what if I were to see you change your mind? What if I saw your ships return to the shores of Carthage? What if you disembark in the midst of the storm and retrace those steps of scorn that led you away from me? Would you call out through the ample rooms of my–of *our* palace?

I gave you everything, starting with myself... I imagine it, hearing your voice scream in a vigorous and eternal plea the name of Dido!

But it will not be so. Who knew that your last gift to me would be despair?

In these interminable moments before the silver thread of my life is cut, I shall remember each scent, each blink of an eye, each hue of the light, each leaf and footprint along the path that lead you to me;

and the path that lead me, be I innocent or guilty, as a plaything of the Gods, or as a being capable of the sovereign will of a woman and a queen, to fuse my soul to yours. But paths can be walked both ways, and there is an infinity on every horizon. You walked away from mine, I shall walk towards it.

And somehow the scent, the wind, the leaf, the footprint, all will reach you like a spear and with as much mercy.

This is the thread of memories that, in the last night of her life, Dido slipped through the eye of the needle of death until she pierced her very heart for Aeneas.

I

I was born in the purple of Tyre. My father was King Belus, my sister was Anna, and Pygmalion was my brother and the beginning of my tragedy.

I was little more than a child when I was betrothed to Sychaeus, the high priest of Melqart, God of Tyre.

When I learnt of my fate I ran into my chambers to cry. Indeed, that seemed just about the only thing I could do. The prospect of marriage was terrifying and the prospect of marrying Sychaeus even more so. That night I could not sleep just thinking that the priest often slit the throats of children and placed their bleeding bodies on the blazing arms of the statue of his God.

Many years after our marriage, Sychaeus confided to me that he detested that part of the ritual. And yet it was necessary. It was material to maintain the balance between the Gods and men.

During my tender years, I would often wane white with fear at the prospect of finding myself embraced by those divine arms. The eclipse of the Gods would overpower my feeble light and I would be consumed in their holy fire.

The pain of those who were given the horror to honour the God was felt everywhere. It was an eternal kind of pain. When the prospect of being chosen hovered above us like a vulture or a halo, mother would hold me to her chest and on her brow, I would see the strange shadows of fear and black terror that shone out of her mind. How different were these images to the scenes of luxury and joy that made up our daily life at court in Tyre.

Tyre, the city south of Phoenicia. Luxurious Tyre. The ever-changing Tyre, Tyre of Our Lord Melqart, of Our Lady Anat, of imperial dye and beauty, of infant death staining the altars with blood; of ships and mariners, tar and the smell of salt; taverns and Tanit, Goddess of the moon, she of the white and silver arms.

'Tanit,' I screamed into the sky that same night of fear and sorrows, 'do not let me be married to Sychaeus. I abhor the priest and his bloodstained hands. Too many years lie between us twain like an abysm of humanity; he is an old man... And I am in love... with a dream. A warrior or a prince, he lives in a far-away land, where the wind crashes like the billows of the sea against high-towered walls, and the moonlight grows on the granite like an exotic flower. A cloak of mist covers his face and a golden band transforms his curly locks into a fountain of frozen bronze. His eyes are grey and when he looks out into the horizon and the sea, they change into the colour of Time. Tanit, sweet Goddess, do not let me be married to Sychaeus.'

A cloud eclipsed Tanit's silvered visage. And yet somehow I knew that the Goddess had heard my prayers and that she would not forget the song of my dreams.

I, however, did have to forget. That is the first step for remembering.

Father decided that I was to become Sychaeus' wife during the summer solstice. Mother would cry but she would obey as well. I vowed that upon becoming a woman, I would never allow myself to bewail a sorrow. I would never allow the world to bring tears and only tears out of me; no, I would become as flint, and the blows of Fortune would create fire from my pain. I would burn my enemies, if nothing else. But o, Aeneas, you made me an enemy to myself.

Mother stroked my hair and told me that my future husband was a good man, a rich man, a descendant from one of the most ancient lineages of Tyre.

I realised that much one afternoon when father and he discussed the terms of the marriage. My brother Pygmalion was with the two of them, as my father wanted to initiate him into the art of government. Sychaeus spoke about how his family had hoarded riches since the days of Hiram, about how there had always been an important priest in his family at every point in history since history itself.

The common people, always thankful for the miracles Sychaeus' forebears had vouchsafed on them, had spent decades ennobling the lineage. He spoke of a treasure. No sooner had the words fallen to the ground like the first drops of rain that I saw the thunderbolt of greed pass through Pygmalion's eyes. And that's when Sychaeus said that the treasure was not to be his. The soothsayers had proclaimed that it was destined from the very beginning of time to finance the construction of city built atop a promontory, a city built in honour of Melqart.

Father furrowed his brow.

'What exactly do these soothsayers mean by that?' he asked.

A slight smile came over Sychaeus' features. That was the first moment I saw something I liked in him. His beard was decorated with silver and his eyes were alive though encaged by his long lashes. He must have been a very handsome man when he was young.

'Soothsayers are seldom exact in their predictions, King Belus.'

'We have discussed the need to found a new colony with the aristocrats. The Assyrians are driving us away from our shores and towards the west. They overwhelm us with demands of tribute and Tyre will never be rich enough to match their voracity.'

'Then it appears that the soothsayers and the aristocrats agree, my king. Tyre must father a new city and be betrothed to the future.'

'But who is to undertake such a mission? Who will brave the dangers of the sea and sail towards nothingness?'

Sychaeus simply shrugged.

'Not us. That is for sure. We have grown too old for such adventures. Maybe a new generation will take

Tyre and its treasure towards the uncharted fortune that awaits it in the west.'

'Meanwhile,' said Pygmalion, who had thereto remained quiet, 'this treasure…'

'Will remain under my watch, as it has so far,' said Sychaeus curtly.

I was not to see my betrothed until the day of the wedding. Distracted as I was with the arrangements for the festivities, with the making of the beautiful dress I was to wear, enamoured by the diadem that the princesses of Tyre carry on their heads and by the prospect of a new life, I ceased beseeching Tanit to impede my marriage to the priest. The night before the wedding, however, I dreamt again about my prince of mist.

He bade me farewell from a distance as I ran towards him, trying to speak my feelings into actions, trying to voice my soul and scream my desire, but instead of running into his arms, I soon reached a cliff. The sea roared and his bireme sailed away until it got lost in a dreamstorm. The wedding was magnificent, the gifts opulent. The maidens of Tyre sang hymns in honour of Anat, and prayed that the Gods keep me fertile. They bathed us with a shower of wheat and I left my parents' home to live with my husband.

When he first removed the veil that covered my face and I saw my own features reflected in his eyes as though in a live looking glass, I knew that I was beautiful. Since that day and night, Sychaeus was nothing but a gentle and loving husband. I even forgot that once he had killed children and offered their lifeless bodies to our stone-eyed, iron-armed Gods.

II

Time passed and those Gods who should have made me fertile remained deaf and dumb. Their eyes of stone saw into my womb and hardened it. Never did I cradle a child or heard one call me mother. Never was I asked to assuage tears or terrors and never did I lift in my arms a child's joy.

At my age, most of the women of Tyre already had three or four children. I was seventeen, and, not having the dues of motherhood to busy myself with, I was able to focus on other affairs. I helped Sychaeus manage his estate and helped father devise strategies to keep the Assyrians away–or, at least, satisfied– with the tributes and gifts we constantly sent their way.

Father was growing old and it was soon time for him to name his heir. Pygmalion never doubted for a second that it was he who was to inherit the throne, but King Belus soon made him realise how wrong he was.

It happened during a visit to Sidon. When we arrived at the baths that stand in the boundaries between the two opulent cities like a bridge between two different glories, our destinies changed. At a gathering where resinated wine flowed copiously and relaxed our spirits, father placed his hands on the heads of his two most-beloved children, and with a timorous voice, already nearing death, already staring into the face of silence, he announced that Pygmalion and I were both to be his successors and that we were to reign together.

'This way,' he said, 'I may die in peace and my shadow will travel across the river of death in a raft of hope. I will see you both prosperous and merry and the Gods themselves will be on your side thanks to the piety of Sychaeus. Then, when Pygmalion takes a wife and begets an heir, the last spark of my soul will melt into the eternal light of Melqart.'

When I was a child, I had always thought with fear and sorrow about the death of those whom I loved best, and yet I knew that death was just another facet of Tanit. However, when I saw my father's sweet visage peeking over my shoulder into the invisible mirror that death held for him even then, sorrow overtook me and I cried on his chest. Pygmalion clenched his jaws and fists and said nothing, but I could tell that the prospect of ruling with me and therefore alongside Sychaeus did not please him at all. I knew that he wanted to be the only one to sit on the throne that Belus would soon leave empty. After all, he had reigned before us all on his own.

'Wipe those tears off your face, my dearest Dido,' he said to me. 'Never cry again; you are a queen and you must rule over those passions that dominate your subjects, just like you must rule over them. Let neither hatred nor love overwhelm you and look at yourself in the silver mirror of the Goddess so that your visage takes on the features of Justice.'

'Father,' said Pygmalion, 'I will honour my sister, and your will will always be the law.'

'Follow always her counsel. Women know better how to smooth out the rough edges of politics, way better than men do. Just like the daring of the latter is what makes cities grow. With both my children on the throne, Tyre's fame will reach beyond the stars.'

He died one month later. My mother Elisa, and Anna, my little sister, cried disconsolately. Remembering my father's words, I covered my face with the saffron-coloured veil I had worn at my wedding and I spilt not one tear. I thought about how Belus was already in the fields of essence, about how he had already begun his journey to become light, or God, or fire; and it was my acts now that would etch his divinity into stone.

Sychaeus lead the funeral procession; the dirges and threnody that honoured father's regal soul that was even now melting into the ether ascended the heavens like a wall-climbing ivy, but Belus would not be cremated but interred. His body would be laid on the earth from east to west, to signal with his temporary form the path of light his eternity would take each day.

Father did not think a proper crowning ceremony for Pygmalion and I was necessary. He wanted the same consistency that he held so dear in his life to live after him: his was a reign of administrators, not tyrants. Phoenician rulers were as far from the pharaohs of Egypt and the kings of Assyria as the stars were from every single one of us. Tyre was inhabited mostly by farmers, fishmongers, and sailors, and so we were more of a mind to produce and promote trade than to conquest and rule over others.

After father had been gone for forty days, Pygmalion told me he wanted to speak to me in private on a matter of utmost importance to the wellbeing of our city.

'As you know,' he said without any dalliance as he sat on the throne, our throne, 'the Assyrians keep pestering all Phoenician cities. The more we give them, the more they want. I have been informed that they expect us to double our tribute. Biblos refuses to pay, and so does Beritos. Sidon remains undecided–in sooth they have enjoyed a period of unmatched prosperity, and they are loath to part with their riches. It is starting to look as though the Assyrians want to provoke us into attacking them. That would demand retaliation, or even worse, the military occupation of our city.'

'We could pay them off,' I told my brother. 'Peace is worth it; that was always father's policy.'

'All must change now,' he said curtly. 'Father was an old man, docile, not warlike like the times demand. Younger blood now rules the state, now runs through its veins and arteries.

'I want to do things differently. I want to strengthen our army, and for once and all crush the Assyrians threat for good.'

'You know that is impossible right now.

'We need gold and we have spent all of our coffers in paying tributes and financing expeditions to found new colonies. That has always been our strength and it must continue to be so.'

'Listen to me, sister, the time has finally come to shake off that Assyrian yoke. The time has come for a new time, for a new era. The future stretches a hand out to us, but we can't reach it if we are chained to our traditions. Now, about the money. You and I both know where we can get it from. I want you to ask Sychaeus for his gold. He will not deny you anything.'

'I myself am not on board. Sychaeus is even less disposed to side with you. He thinks like father did. That treasure, as he has told me, as he has told *us*, is destined to finance a Tyrian city unlike anything the world has ever seen. And that will happen, as he told me, as he told *us*, when the Gods decree it. You wish to steal from the future to give your vanity a present. Sychaeus at least understands that there is a time for history.'

A thunderbolt of fury passed through my brother's eyes. I could tell he was trying his hardest to rule over his passions.

'Enough, Dido! The world cannot be ruled based on what the entrails of oxen or the discarded feathers of birds tell us! Don't you realise it is all a lie? The Gods do not speak to us, they do not appear to us, they do not care about us at all. If they demand sacrifices and gold, they do so through the voices of the priests, who are just as vain and ambitious as every other man, in every other time and every other land. Do you or don't you know where Sychaeus keeps his treasure?'

'No. And I do not mean to ask him. I advise you to speak to him directly. I cannot come between the two of you, because I am his wife, and because, unlike you, I think that that treasure belongs to the Gods and to the temple. I also do not think that we should militarise Tyre and become something that we are not. Trade, travel and expansion, that's what we are, what Tyre is, just like all of the other Phoenician cities. Despite the belligerence of other peoples, the Assyrians, the Persians, the Egyptians, despite them all, we have always managed to live and thrive in peace, facing the sea and tilling the land.'

Even as I spoke, I realised that I was growing agitated and that I was about to lose that equanimity and serenity that father had tasked always to keep in mind. My brother looked at me with a coldness that would soon turn to molten hatred, and I understood how difficult it would be for us to rule together. We were just too different from one another.

III

The gold and ruby columns of the temple of Melqart glittered in the light. Forced by the dignity of our office, Pygmalion and I had to attend a sacrificial ceremony. A few days before, Sychaeus had announced that a *moloch* was necessary. There was no escaping it, we needed to sacrifice a child in order to repel the Assyrians for just a little while longer.

Before that day, I didn't doubt that that's what the Gods demanded. Such cruelty could only be divine, for it never occurred to me that men are the true monsters of the world.

Pygmalion clenched his teeth and threw me a savage look. On my part, I was confused. I was disgusted at the fact that such a tiny creature had to die in so cruel a manner, and what's more, before the eyes of the whole city, before the eyes of his own mother, who, to make matters worse, had to maintain a dignified and even insouciant expression. She had to feel honoured that her son would be given over to the Gods.

According to Sychaeus, the Gods had never failed to deliver, and, without exception, after the sacrifice, the Assyrians always left our shores and went to ravage other lands.

Other lands? Biblos? Sidon? Beritos? All Phoenician cities, all sister cities that would also offer their citizens as sacrifice to fend off the invaders, just as we ourselves did. And so? How could it work, 'without exception?'

This time, the honoured victim was a girl. She was a tiny thing, no more than four years old. She arrived in the temple cradled by her mother. Upon seeing them, I remembered my childhood fears, that terror I suffered at the prospect of being sacrificed to the God myself.

We exited the temple and walked in silence towards the altar, towards that dais that overwhelmed us with feelings of dread because of what had and was to happen there. That was the *tofet*, but a word could never stand for the horror that took place in it.

Often the human victim would be substituted by a lamb... but not on this most foredooming of days. The Gods would accept nothing but a human being if they were to bring peace to Tyre and drive away the Assyrian menace.

I wished to be on the other side of the world, living or burning in the sun or atop a star. I would not allow myself to look at the face of this soon-to-be-childless mother, or at the hands of my husband who even now was holding a knife over a defenceless throat. First he would slit it, so that Melqart could receive the blood in his arms; then the body would be burnt like human incense, and the smoke would eventually reach the voracious appetites of the God. I remembered how Pygmalion spoke of the Gods as if they were not even real. It was too terrible to even consider that. If the Gods did not exist, then that would make all of these sacrifices all the more terrible, all the more senseless… if the Gods did not exist then that would make perfect sense.

Finally, the ceremony reached its end. Sychaeus washed his hands. The child's mother was dragged away by her relations. She had lost consciousness, too much pain can do that to a person. I imagined how intolerable life would seem to her when she woke up. If that had happened to me, I would not be able to embrace my husband again: between the two of us there would always be the shadow of our child, still dripping black blood from its throat.

Instead of returning home with Sychaeus, I visited my parents' house. There I found my sister, as overwhelmed as I was by the horror we had all borne witness to in the *tofet*.

'The elders speak that it's time to sail for a new city,' Anna said in a whisper, 'I wish I could be a part of that expedition and colony. I would explain to them that sacrificing children is not necessary. We should give only lambs or birds to the Gods.'

I took her hand in mine. I had often indulged in the same idea. A new Tyre, over the horizon and sea, not haunted by the shadow of human sacrifice. Was it possible?

I spent the night in my old home and slept in Anna's room. That was the only way I could escape the nightmares. When I woke up, I realised I did not want to sleep under the same roof as Sychaeus anymore, even if he was a good man in other aspects of his life; even if he loved me; even if he made my life a comfortable one. Seeing in my mind how he slit the throat of that girl made me hate him. I sighed when I realised that my hatred changed nothing.

There is no divorce in Tyre, and the services a woman owes to her husband constitute a bond stronger than adamantine. There was no escape from it, I would be his until death did us part.

Inside the palace, there was a strange atmosphere; it was almost as if everyone were expecting a messenger to arrive with black news. Anna seemed tired and remained quiet all the while. I drifted through the rooms of my childhood and arrived at the main hall of the palace, where so many times I had seen my father entertaining his royal guests and where I now shared the throne with Pygmalion.

In that moment, a servant from my own retinue came to meet me with downcast eyes.

'My queen, may the Gods have mercy on us.'

'What is the matter? Speak.'

'Your royal husband has been murdered, my lady. He was found next to the altar of Melqart with his throat slit.'

I felt like I was drowning. I felt guilty, almost as if I myself had wielded the dagger that cut his life in twain. Sychaeus. To think that I had wished never to see him again! horrified as I was by his priestly office and homicidal hands. But I never wished for him to die! He was my husband. He was… he is not anymore.

I could not think clearly, I had no perception but a hailstorm of details. I remembered the dead girl and her mother and the most minuscule of events of the previous day. I could see everything closely, much too closely, as though the curtains of time and proximity had been blown open by a violent breeze: a crack in the road that took us to the *tofet*, a wrinkle in Anna's tunic. Sychaeus. He is dead. Had his body been already carried away?

That's when Pygmalion entered the hall.

'I have just heard what has happened, and I grieve with you, sister. Tragedy has come over Tyre. The Gods were not appeased by the sacrifice we offered them. Other measures must be taken.'

'Who could have done this bloody deed, Pygmalion? He has been murdered! But he had no enemies. His exuberance and disposition made him a well-loved man. He was held in the highest esteem by all of Tyre!'

'We all have enemies, Dido. All of us. Some hide where we least expect it; some are made in an instant, by a rash decision or some hollow words. We will take care of the funeral ceremony. Now you must tell me where he hid the treasure. Whoever killed him did so to get to his gold, that much we know for sure. We must get there before him.'

'I told you I don't know.'

Pygmalion grabbed me by the shoulders and looked deep into my eyes. After a while he let me go.

'I believe you,' he said coldly. 'We must rummage through his house. We must go through every room and passage until we find it.'

'What if he hid it in the temple?'

Pygmalion did not answer. He ran out of our late father's palace and I was left alone to grieve in silence the death of my husband, the pious Sychaeus, high priest of Melqart.

IV

I could not then give in to tears. And I can't do it now, Aeneas, for dear that I will drown the fire burning under me.

I had to arrange Sychaeus' obsequies. Pain and fear besieged the city and a never-ending parade of mourners marched in funerary rites before the body of its high priest. That day, I saw the mother of the child that the God or my late husband had taken in the funeral procession. Her child was dead. Now so was my husband, and in the horizon the Assyrian sails infected the sun. All for nothing? It was like being in a painful dream. Death had taken over the city; Tyre's purple heart was almost crushed into pieces.

I could not sleep for three days. Anna told me Pygmalion had excavated under the temple hoping to find the treasure… And all of his efforts had been in vain. Yet, the treasure was real, and it had to be somewhere.

This, nevertheless, did not concern me for the moment; I was far too busy trying to put everything back into some semblance of an order. Sychaeus' unexpected demise had left uncountable affairs in a state of grievous disarray and I decided to take them on with no loss of time; this was also made possible by the immense help given me by Kenfas, my late husband's secretary.

Reading Sychaeus' tablets, I soon understood that most of his work had been dedicated to planning out this famous new city. In one of his tablets he had even got so far as to picking a place for this future colony. It lay to the west, past the stars and the legends of our past dreams. The west was a great choice: there were few or none warlike peoples in that direction and the areas we could settle were close to the sea and therefore graced by amiable climes.

Another tablet showed me the interest with which Sychaeus followed the development of the Trojan War. In the Hellespont, to the north, it was said that the Grecian powers had besieged a powerful trade centre for ten years. Troy had finally fallen, as we had learnt not long ago by the horrific narratives of the visiting aoidos that often graced us with their tales at court. Troy had fallen like a star. It had seemed so far away a few months ago, and when we learnt that its towers had been totalled and now lay on the ground like the skeletons of giants, we all wondered whether the heavens would crush us.

From Troy, from that bleeding city, it was said that a group of fugitives had escaped during the cover of night and ash. At the head of this troop was Prince Aeneas, son of Anchises and a Goddess; this warrior was divinely tasked with taking the penates of Troy and the sacred Palladium to a new city he himself would build. The augurs were their usual ambiguous selves. This new city would rise in Crete, or perhaps in Africa, or maybe in the fertile lands of dream-like Hesperia.

My late husband, on the other hand, did not allow fur such oracular ambiguity. He had chosen the exact place where this new Tyrian city would rear its walls and temples and salute the sun. Based on intelligence gathered by Phoenician sailors, he had decided this new Tyre would be built in a spot of land where a promontory created a natural citadel–like that of Athens or of Troy– and it would stand with the African deserts to its back, proudly facing the sea.

After Sychaeus had been dead for five nights, weary of reading his tablets, I went to sleep on what used to be our bed. Tired as I was, sleep did not come easily for me, until it did.

Two proud gates, one of ivory and one of horn stand in that land of infinite space where the immortal Gods think, know, and play us into existence. How was I to know that that night I would dream a dream of horn?

Sychaeus walked up to me, with an expression of most-dejected sorrow and a purple tunic, dyed in blood. One of his hands was pressed to his throat, as if he were trying to assuage some terrible pain or keep himself from spilling over.

I knew it was a dream, but I also knew that I was truly in front of his shadow.

'Dido,' said he, 'I have come to bid farewell to you, to you, my loving and loved wife, to you who lavished me with happiness and tenderness all those days granted me by the Gods.

'I don't have much time to talk to you; shadow as I am, I lack the strength of the living. I wish I could embrace you, but I cannot; to plant a kiss on your silky hair is a dream that dream men cannot longer have.

'But now I will reveal a terrible truth that will harrow up your soul. Your brother, killed me. He sought to pry away from my life the secret of my gold. Ambition turned him into a rabid hound and filled him with unmercy. He desecrated Melqart's altar when he spilled my sacred blood on the God's image. As I lay dying, I told him the gold was buried under the very same sacred ground he had polluted. But that was a lie. When he excavated under the God, he damned himself.

'But now I will tell the truth to you, so that you can use the treasure to leave Tyre forever. Take whomever you think remains loyal to you, and build a new city. Travel, travel until you face the sea and give your back to the deserts of Africa, and settle our new Tyre in the name of Melqart.

'It shall prosper, the Gods have granted us that much. It might even be eternal. This shall be her name, listen closely, my Dido, my queen, my beloved wife, *Qart Hadasht,* Carthage, the new city.

'Now, to find the treasure you will need to be brave, braver than you have ever been. You will need to face those fears that were your childhood, that disgust at the injunctions of divinity, its hunger for children and lambs of whiteness. The treasure, my queen, is buried under the *tofet.* There, in that self-same place where

34

just a few days ago you saw me horror-struck as I slit the throat of that girl Melqart had taken for himself.

'To get to the treasure you will have to withstand the sight of sacrifice, of blanched bones, and silent skulls, and of death itself, my Dido. You need to face this death so that you can take your life and faith in our Gods to the African shores, where the proud name of Carthage and Dido will clamour through the granite halls of eternity.'

V

I awoke from my dream with both a sorrowful and a resolved heart. Sychaeus had crossed the mists of death to point his finger at the culprit, to disclose to me the hiding place of his gold, and to crown me queen of a new city. There was no question about it, it was my duty to honour his memory and to find a strength within myself worthy of his; How to do that? After all, he had stormed the bulwarks that separate the living from the dead.

Aurora had not yet gilded the visage of the heavens when I roused Kenfas from sleep. I knew I could trust my purpose to him. Four loyal servants joined us and before dawn broke we made our way towards the temple of Melqart and through the garden until at last we reached the *tofet*.

I made it a point of remaining there while the servants used their instruments to break the earth open. I stayed with them throughout the whole process to follow the sable injunctions of the shadow and to overcome the test of death. The carbonised bones of a myriad victims appeared after the first swings of the pickaxes. White bones played in counterpoint to them. I placed my hand on my chest, yet I did not close my eyes; rather I saw the ineffable face of my people's religion.

In that moment, I stopped being afraid. I could feel a new Dido being born inside me. I left behind the frightened child, and the young woman that prayed to Tanit; I was now queen Dido, who prayed to herself. Until I saw you, Aeneas, and I prayed to your mother.

Underneath the ossuary, we found a chest of considerable size. I gave commands and it was lifted, and, after returning the bones to the bosom of the earth, we carried the chest to Sychaeus' home.

I had a busy morning. I sent surreptitious missives to some of the noble families of Tyre that I trusted would want to join me in this most glorious enterprise. I bade them meet me at the docks in three days' time to sail away on the briny flood. I denied audience to Pygmalion. At first he assumed that I was broken with pain for Sychaeus' death. This deception did not last all forever, and one day he disregarded my wishes and entered my rooms in a fury. He found me going over Sychaeus' tablets with Kenfas, whom he dismissed peremptorily.

'Stop all of this nonsense, Dido. As your king, I demand that you surrender the treasure of Sychaeus over to me.'

'Was it not enough to have murdered him?' I asked him drily. I could see his face go white with fear.

'Who told you such nonsense?'

'Sychaeus himself came to me in a dream and lifted the veil of mortal ignorance to show me your deceptions. You are a murderer and you do not deserve to rule over Tyre.'

'Hold your tongue, serpent. If by this time tomorrow you do not send your servants to my palace with the treasure, I will order your arrest and the executioners will pry the secret from you alongside your tongue.'

Pygmalion stormed out in a formidable rage. His threats had not scared me, and I understood that I was the owner of a new fortitude, something I had chiselled out of my own self: a soul of stone.

I sent for my mother and sister to take them with me, but mother refused to leave Tyre. We knew we would never see each other again, and we held each other one last time, wrapped in a veil of sorrow and death. Mother, the past queen Elisa, was torn to shreds when she learnt from me that her very own son had murdered my husband in cold blood. I, the future queen Dido, was ripped apart at the prospect of leaving forever. But I was forced to set aside my feelings and my pain and sail for an unreal city, founded by the shadow of a dead man, in the shadow of a future plunged into the mist of the sea.

Anna likewise bewailed our leaving mother behind, but her soul was resolved.

'I will walk by your side through the paths of life and death, Dido. Our destinies are forever knit together, and you will be my queen in your new city.'

The next morning the docks were teeming with life. It had been impossible to conceal our going away, and, even though I had commanded silence to those I had chosen to take with me, the rumour had reached upwards of eighty noble families. They all had sent their youths to accompany me with their ambition and hearts on fire: it was as though the Gods themselves had planned my departure.

The weather was auspicious, the sea calm; the biremes were laden with victuals, furniture, jewellery, rich cloths, tools, and animals. The dark days that had taken over Tyre were over and now light reigned anew. The sea was azure, as were my hopes. The decorations on the ships were purple as was the passion and pride of Tyre at the prospect of sailing out to sea in an expedition of immense daring. Phoenicians and sailors that we are, adventure runs in our blood.

The life of Tyre left the palaces and temples and moved towards the great unknown, as blood leaves a sacrificed victim and pools in the altar, and the city itself seemed to expand and walk with Goddess-like steps through the main.

No sooner had Anna, Kenfas and I boarded the ship that held my late husband's treasure than Pygmalion's army made an appearance at the docks. Panic ran amuck through the throngs of people. Some perished under the hoofs of horses, others transfixed by the swords Pygmalion had unleashed on his own people. Others, however, ran towards the biremes and saved both life and property.

If Pygmalion decided to chase us through the waves, we were resolved to fight until death tamed us. But however long we stared out into the horizon, we never saw trace of the Tyrian murderer. Hours slipped past themselves and confidence in our enterprise blew kind winds on our sails. The cloth was filled with our dreams and the mean rowed with the desire of living through leaving everything behind. At one point, a dolphin surfaced in front of our ship and its jovial acrobatics kept us company for a while. I smiled, and so did the Gods.

But time rots everything, Aeneas. And that same pearl smile I wore tastes of ashes now that you are gone.

The die was cast. At sea we were fenced in by nothing but the stars above us and our future ahead of us. We made sacrifices to Melqart and whenever it was my turn to pour libation, I would feel the ether change. I thought about Aeneas, that Trojan prince whose fortune I had read on Sychaeus' tablets. He too had been forced to leave behind his natal city; he too had trusted his destiny to the bellied promise of a bireme and the will of the Gods.

VI

Soon we sighted the shores of Cyprus, that same isle that saw the birth of Aphrodite. We traced the hourglass curves of her shoreline and we finally landed in Paphos. Many members of the Cyprian nobility and their kind gestures presaged a fruitful future to our desires. Almost immediately after arriving in Paphos, I made my way to the temple of Aphrodite; upon seeing the young girls that sat on the steps to the temple, honouring the custom to offer themselves to foreigners for one night, I felt a daring idea take hold of my mind.

It is well known that no man can spend a night in Paphos without yielding to passion. The very columns of the temple to the foam-born Goddess seem to quiver under the atmosphere of sensuality and love: they can barely stand straight giving in to their own desires. Pleasure is the chiefest trade in that city. Commerce comes in second place, and war is not considered at all.

It's all part of a tradition rich in history. Maybe it started with Cinyras and Myrrha, from their love was

Adonis born; that same Adonis that would so inflame Aphrodite herself. After that, the kings of Cyprus gave their daughters away in marriage and yet the power of mothers has never quite left this isle of bronze.

I sought to have an audience with whomever it was that managed the affairs of the temple. A priest with an argent beard and black locks of hair received me with all the pomp and circumstance due to a queen. He reminded me ever so slightly of Sychaeus. His name was Khalkos and he confessed it was his duty to give in to all of the desires of Queen Dido.

'How do you know my name?' I asked him in disbelief.

'The winds travel faster than men do. They are the most efficient messengers. I also know that the Tyrian fleet that escorts you is tasked with founding a new city.'

'I wanted your advice on that, and your help. The flower of youth still blossoms about me, but very few women came with me in the bellied biremes. Eighty Tyrian families sent their youths in this glorious expedition. That is the number of maidens I would require of this temple and of Aphrodite herself. They shall be honoured in the new city we will build in the coasts of Africa.'

'If we grant you that boon, your city would be a daughter of Aphrodite.'

'I call her Tanit. She is my Goddess. I often see her in the moon and in the pearls that hang from my ears.'

'Aphrodite, Astarte, Tanit, Venus,' said the priest under his breath, 'all of these names are worthy of worship, and all refer to a mighty Goddess. Powerful and dreadful. Aphrodite has a warm countenance from which shine forth both pleasure and delight, but she is also the source of the most direful distress, and she herself has driven unnumbered souls to the very gates of death, to graves and pyres. Do not let that happen to you, Queen Dido.'

'I worship the Goddess, but as a woman I'm not within her reach... I have pledged myself to the memory of my late husband, Sychaeus, and never will I love another man again.'

'In matters of love, "never" is just another word, Queen Dido. The fires of passion can burn a body just as completely as a soul. As priest to this temple I advise you not to anger the Goddess. Today you shall sacrifice a white lamb in her honour, that she may forgive your rash words. She rules over you–over all of us– do not forget that.'

'She cannot rule over queens, o wise one. I owe loyalty to the ideals of dead men, to human spirits and not human beings. Belus, my father, who wished nothing but to extend the spirit of Tyre through land and sea; Sychaeus, who never stopped dreaming that dream until he became one.

'Nevertheless, you are right. Aphrodite is powerful indeed, and today I will sacrifice a lamb to every letter in her name, be it Tanit or Astarte; she was born in the foam and Paphos is her native land. And I humbly beseech you to provide me with eighty maidens from her temple who will turn into the mothers of the first citizens of Carthage.'

'Allow me to speak a prophecy, Queen Dido. I can see into the future and in this moment I can feel the prophetic fires within me swell to a burning rage.'

'Tell me, o wise one. Simple mortal that I am, the voice of the Gods is forbidden me; prophets like you are blessed indeed.'

Khalkos' pupils were fixed and glassy; each particular hair on his body now stood on end and his voice became harsh and deep. A mysterious zephyr shook the thickets of his soul and a will stronger than his own now spoke the future onto me.

'A man will transfix your life, come from death and fire, bringing death and fire. But Carthage shall be eternal for a thousand years, until those come from death and fire destroy it and they themselves return to the whiteness of their bones.'

I felt my whole frame shake. I thought about the *tofet,* the blanched bones of all the children who had died there. I thought about Sychaeus and his murder. A man come from death and fire. Who? When?

You, you. It is easy to look back on the past and point at the inevitable, Aeneas, but who could have known back then? Who in the middle of the first act of her own tragedy, can know of the dramatic irony that awaits her?

And yet the oracle promised a thousand years of eternity. Innumerable generations, and their seeds were here; rash Phoenician youths that had by now disembarked from the air-like ships; and in front of me, beautiful maidens sitting on the steps to the temple, with their white tunics looking like foam in the sunlight.

Driven by the invisible influence of the Goddess, some Phoenician youths had already placed coins and necklaces and earrings made of gold, on the laps of the most beautiful maidens as they uttered the words 'I invoke the Goddess in you.'

Eager to partake in this Tyrian birth–for our city's fame had crossed the wine-coloured main a long time ago–the other girls did not refuse when they were called by Khalkos. I felt glad for the least beautiful amongst them; were it not for this boon of love, they would have had to wait days and months, maybe even years, until some foreign traveller cared to place a coin on their lap.

Those same biremes that had sailed form Tyre in an effort to escape Pygmalion's soldiers had now metamorphosed into conjugal barges of pleasure. During our time at sea the air resounded with Cyprian song, sweet hymns in honour of Aphrodite swam alongside us, and glided through the sky in auspicious dances. Riotous Phoenician lays went deeper into the main than our oars, and maybe they even reached the ear of the old man of the sea and Triton and the nereids of argent hair. Our Tyrian nightmare had become a dream of hope and we reached the shores of Africa with no further trouble.

VI

Before he died, Sychaeus had heard of a peninsula fenced in by the Mediterranean and a lake. This site also featured a promontory that would serve as a magnificent and natural coign of vantage. On his tablets, he also wrote that this land of dream was not ripe for the taking. It belonged to a Libyan tribe called the Gaetili, a warlike people governed by King Jarbas.

We could not simply leave our ships and start raising our pavilions. First, we had to ask the king to give us leave. We were prepared to buy the land if it came to it; after all, that's why we had brought the treasures of Tyre with us. Nevertheless, for centuries, the natural disposition of our race, made stronger by our propensity for trade and bargaining, has taught us to be wary and never to name a prize but to wait until one is named. Why buy the land if it was perhaps possible to get it for free? In the long run, our presence in Africa would benefit everyone: a peaceful Phoenician settlement would revitalise the almost non-existent trade routes between the Gaetili and other tribes.

The prestige of Tyre was enough for anyone to want us as a neighbouring state.

I came to King Jarbas in the traditional habit of a Phoenician princess; my arms were bedecked with golden bracelets and long earrings hung from my earlobes.

The king, a Berbers monarch, lived in the wild luxury of his nomadic tent. He lay extended on sumptuous cushions, with an ornate censer at his feet and guarded by fierce-looking warriors. He reminded me of those haughty men who, astraddle their camels, traverse the deserts in their way to Judea while they scrutinise the stars and heavens.

Jarbas was a tall man with bright eyes and of a swarthy complexion. I addressed him accompanied by Kenfas and two noble young Phoenicians. I told him who I was and waited for him to commence the rites of hospitality. For a moment, he seemed to hesitate. Maybe he thought I was an impostor, or perhaps a high-ranking woman in this environment of warriors and sand was something of which he could not conceive. Nevertheless, he overcame his initial doubts and soon behaved as it behoved a Libyan king at an audience with one as myself.

'If you will allow me to express my most immediate thoughts, I must confess that the queen of Tyre is certainly beautiful. Nothing would please me better than to indulge you on your every want and need. But I'm afraid that first I will need to know what these are.'

After saying this he lifted a date from a silver tray and offered it to me. I took it from his hand, bit into the rich flesh of the fruit and smiled at my host who even now regarded me with passion in his eyes.

'My wishes, o king, are to rejoice in the grandeur of your land and to pay homage to your very stars. In the name of the Gods of Tyre, we beseech you for a piece of your land and for your friendship.'

'My friendship is already yours, Queen Dido. Now as to the matter of land, we do not possess as much as you would think. Our sovereignty over these regions is oft disputed by other Libyan peoples.'

'We do not ask for much, noble King. Our numbers are few and only eighty Tyrian houses have embarked upon this African enterprise with me. We wish only to rear a new city under the protection of Melqart, and to turn it into our home. I assure you, its glory will awe everyone who travels through these lands.'

Jarbas did not stop looking at me and I started to feel anxious. It was obvious that I had stirred forgotten passions within him and that would not help me in bargaining for what I came for. I glanced over at his warriors and guards and I experienced a vague feeling of apprehension. Kenfas and I were at his mercy. That is when the shrewd secretary made his way into the conversation.

'We do not wish to be the cause behind any mischance in your dominions, o noble King. If our presence could lead to any misfortune, we will seek another place to build our city. We will sail for Hesperia; as other Phoenician ships have done in the past. We only chose the shores of Africa because our Gods instructed us to do so.'

51

'That is not the problem. That such a noble queen would choose our humble lands honours the Gaetili. To breach the abyss between words and deeds I hereby grant you those acres of land you asked of me for your glorious purpose.'

Below Jarbas' feet was a *byrsa* made from the hide of an ox. He lifted it from the floor and held it in front of us.

'All of the land that you can enclave within the bounds of this skin shall be yours today.'

Kenfas blinked in disbelief. I myself felt insulted. Was this barbarian mocking us? And yet, I accepted his proposal, for Phoenician cunning had already taken over my mind.

'I humbly thank you, gracious King. Your *boundless* generosity is revealed within the limits of the *byrsa*. At the end of the day, send a supervisor to my ship and you will learn how much land we were able to claim inside your skin.

I could feel Kenfas staring at me. He had guessed how determined I was.

VIII

'I knew that the Phoenicians were astute, but never had I undergone the consequences of their cunning.'

Jarbas had demanded an audience with me as soon as he learnt just how many acres of land we had managed to encompass within the limits of his *byrsa*. All that land, by his own word and honour, was now mine.

'However cunning we may be, it is not too large an area of your kingdom, and let me assure you, o noble one, that we will honour your gift and lift your name and ours towards the very heavens.'

'You cut the skin into the thinnest strips possible to be able to contain a vast expanse of land.'

'The majority of which is the promontory. It will be our citadel and we shall call it Byrsa in honour of your gift.'

The king burst out laughing. He was not moved to a rage, but I could perceive some anxiety lurking in his black eyes. He had been invaded by the peaceful foreigners whom, most child-like, he had taken in with his games.

'The Gods are behind your arrival to our coasts. It has not been in vain that the docks in Tyre now lie empty. Maybe you will hear the hymns of Hymen in these lands, in the palace of a noble prince, or perhaps inside the tent of a powerful king,' he said.

'I have sworn eternal faith to the ashes of my late husband, Sychaeus, o king. I am only here per his injunctions, his last will. And to follow it, never will I take another husband.'

'I understand, Queen Dido. Your loyalty is a virtue. But take my advice: never tell this to anyone again. Your words would incense more than a few Libyan kings and it is only natural to expect embassies from noble suitors sent to win you over.'

Jarbas rose from his seat and covered himself with his cloak. Outside his servants waited for him. He was helped onto his horse and soon he was riding away in a most regal fashion. He had granted me the land I needed for my new city, and that was what mattered. Yet I felt uneasy. I was sure more amatory advances would be soon to come. I would reject them as I had pledged a heap of ash I would, but in the long run, would this not be incredibly detrimental to our eternal sojourn in his kingdom? Yet I would not break my promise. Dido was to reign alone.

Now Dido is to die alone. That promise at least, I will keep, Aeneas.

A few days after he left my ships, I received a present from Jarbas. It was a tripod of fine bronze, inlaid with Grecian gold that did nothing but confirm my fears. Nothing is ever given away without any strings attached, and my stratagem relating to the *byrsa* had made many strings out of a cow's hide.

I was determined not to give in to Jarbas' proposal or to that of any other African nobleman. I poured libation in honour of Sychaeus and the Gods of death.

I forgot to pray to Tanit and payed dearly for it, Aeneas. For Love is the most powerful deity in any world and I had vouched to remain true to a pile of ash.

The men began laying the groundwork for the first constructions of Carthage. A temple to Melqart, who was to shine over the city like a new sun, was now coming out of the east. After that, we would need to build a shipping yard. I had the whole thing in my mind: a semi-circular dream, decorated with proud columns, a true sanctuary to the sea.

Those days of construction, of seeing my city come out of my dreams and into the world were the happiest of my life. I was a mother without the pain: I could not feel exhaustion; I awoke before Aurora broke her roses in the sky; I went to bed at midnight, breathing the perfumed breeze of this new country that would carry in its bosom the name of Phoenicia. This new city, Qart Hadasht, Carthage… it seemed to come from our timeless memories of the future like a deity wrapped in whiteness, a Goddess of both sea and land, of earth and sun to grow towards a destiny of glory.

At the foot of the promontory we would rise our hopes and homes; they would grow towards the sky like the mast of a ship. And so that's where we planted our nostalgia and designed houses after the traditional Tyrian style. However, though the Phoenician shores of old were certainly beautiful, there was just something about the coasts of Libya. There was a charm in the elements that surrounded us, an oasis of light in the air. The colour of the sea has no comparison with anything else in the world, as sailors often say. It is the looking glass of the Gods and their pleasure palace.

It seemed necessary that our story be set down in stone, if only to leave a piece of ourselves in Time and Memory. And so, Kenfas and I inscribed the story of Carthage into tablets, and placed them at the temple of Melqart in Byrsa, next to the story of the Trojan war. The latter had ended a while ago in the Hellespont, with the death of the Trojan princes and the victory of the noble Greeks. The victors were, nonetheless, punished either by traversing the seas in aimless dangers or by finding death itself at familiar hands: wives turned against husbands, brothers against sisters, sons against fathers, thus was the bond of nature smashed into broken despairs. It happened in every kingdom and city from Levant to Hesperia. The bloody deeds of noble hands were re-enacted by the wandering bards, and thus familial feuds and heroic battles were yoked in lays into tales of awe.

The will of the Gods rules over our lives. It is inscrutable, even if everyone, Gods and men, must bow to Destiny, that faceless deity without a name.

In the lights of night and silver moonlight, I yearned after my mother and my childhood, my father's kind character, and my natal home. When I could feel the tears welling up in my eyes, I forced myself to look into the face of the future. I knew that it looked down or back on me and on the birth of Carthage.

The buildings grew from their seeds of quicklime to the promise of heaven. The sculptures that told our tale grew expressions and desires. In the evening, I would walk beside them, accompanied by Anna; next to the tumult and turmoil of the day we sailed away from Tyre, the sculptors had etched into stone scenes from the day Troy was taken: Trojan streets teeming with Greek soldiers, engendered in the womb of a horse of wood, the stratagem of Ulysses, King of Ithaca.

I saw my features on a statue. I and it wore a veil that was to be dyed with imperial purple. I saw myself going into the bellied bireme, holding to my bosom the effigies of Melqart and Tanit. Next to me I could see Prince Aeneas, you, my Aeneas, carrying your father Anchises over your shoulder. In your hands, you held the Penates of your natal city.

IX

The months sped past us. Occasionally, we were graced with missives and presents sent by other African kings who wanted to annex my new city to their dominions. The thought of it, their barbarian tribes and my Carthage, their hands and mine made me tremble. Jarbas, however, did not importune me again after he sent the tripod and I even got to thinking the Berber king had changed his mind.

If he were to grace my court with his presence again, I would offer him Anna's hand if only to demonstrate our gratitude. He simply could not refuse that gesture and Anna would be a very convenient match for him. Besides, she had a favourable opinion towards the king and it was time for her to be married.

But I was not familiar with the ways and minds of these African noblemen. I soon learnt that their affections were not sedentary and that they could not accept sovereign sway to be held by a woman.

Jarbas had wanted to have his fun with the newly-arrived foreigner by granting her the hide of an ox, and he had learnt his lesson. His shepherd's joke had

turned into a city and had even named the immense
citadel that he could not but come across whenever he
rode his horse wrapped in his red cloak and Berber
vigour.

In his tablets, Sychaeus had written about planting
grapevines in the new city. The wine of Tyre is
renowned throughout the world, as are the resinated
wines of Sidon and the elixirs of Biblos. Our ships
had been laden with seeds and soon we agreed upon
making a special occasion of the day in which the
first seeds would be swallowed by the ground. The
farmland lay beyond the assigned territory to our
city, but I did not consider it necessary to respect the
imposed boundaries, especially as we would give
King Jarbas the best grapes and the first vintage that
ever came from them.

We were in the midst of sacrificing to the Gods
when I saw the figure of Jarbas stand atop a nearby
hill. He was watching us; even judging by his shadow,
he seemed perfectly aware that we had trespassed
beyond the boundaries that circumscribed us. I
decided to meet him after we finished paying tribute
to the Gods.

I walked towards the foot of the hill alone, but,
upon arriving there, Jarbas did not move. What was
I to do? If I walked up to him, maybe such a gesture
could be construed as obsequious and complaisant.
Nevertheless, I was on his land and it was I who had
commanded the grapevines be planted there. With
such thoughts, I walked up the hill and towards the
king.

'You have broken your word, Queen Dido,' he said to me without getting down from his horse.

'I am sorry, my lord. I shall compensate you for this injury. We shall sow grapevines on your land and ours and we shall teach your people the secrets behind Tyrian wine. It is said it pleases the very Gods.'

'Yesternight I dreamt a terrible dream, Queen Dido. You burnt to death in a pyre and the Gods were joyful for it.'

I felt a cold chill going down my back. Why was he telling me this?

'In my dream,' he continued, 'a moon-made Goddess told me that the only way to prevent your death was for me to marry you. Even if it was against your will.'

I held my peace. Jarbas descended from his horse and placed his hands on my shoulders.

'You have invaded my territory. Now I ask you to invade me. Marry me and all of Libya will be yours. I shall conquer it for you. I will not allow you to perish in the pyre of your Phoenician pride. You mustn't be tied to a dead man's ashes.'

I began trembling. For a few seconds that same fear that I had been able to vanquish in the *tofet* of Tyre, amidst the burnt bones of countless victims, came back to me and stuck in my throat. I was suddenly afraid to die, afraid of burning to death in that pyre of dreams or nightmares. But then I saw the shadow of Sychaeus wearing a most melancholy expression on his face and I was able to quell my spirits.

'I am honoured by your proposal, King Jarbas, but I have sworn dreadful vows to the deities of Death, vows that cannot, that can never be broken. Perhaps you saw my destiny in your dream; perhaps you didn't, for the Gods sometimes send false visions and rejoice in our mistakes and apprehensions. I humbly implore your forgiveness for having crossed the boundaries we agreed upon. This very instant I'll order the plants uprooted and we will manage to get by with the territory you have so graciously granted us.'

'Do you detest me, Queen Dido?'

'Nothing is further away from the truth, King Jarbas. And so that you know this to be the case, I offer to you the hand of my sister, Anna. Imagine it, my king, the Gaetuli and the Phoenicians, all turned into a single blood, thick and red like the wine that our grapes will produce next harvest.'

'I have not dreamt of your sister. I have only dreamt about you. I saw you burning. The Gods sent me that dream to save you, and it was not a false vision. I grew interpreting the wind and deciphering the stars: I can read time and tell apart soft-spoken voices amidst the storms of the desert.'

I raised my hand to interrupt him, but he only took it in his, and placed his other hand upon my lips.

'Do not say anything else. Leave your grapevines where they are.

'But think about my dream and about the future of your Phoenician colony. I know your sister is as beautiful as you are and even younger, but I will only take Dido for a wife.'

Jarbas let go of my hand and got back on his horse. He rode away with a farewell gesture and I felt a strange pressure on my chest, as though that was the moment in which I had started to die.

When I first saw you, Aeneas, I felt like I started to live.

X

We kept on building, even as the grapevines kept on growing. Some of us took to the shores to search for the murex, the mollusc of the imperial dye. In the meantime, we imported fabrics from all of the Phoenician cities, except from Tyre…

Pygmalion's intensions to pursue us were cut short by the Assyrians. The vague menace of old had been ossified into a foreign presence in the Tyrian streets. Strange warriors had taken over the city, and killed the men and enslaved the women. The messengers that reported such a tragedy could barely look me in the eyes as they narrated the cruel contents of their myriad messages.

My mother had died in the first skirmish. She threw herself off a terrace to avoid a harsher fate. My brother had managed to escape, though whither bound was unknown.

A black mist settled over Anna and me when we learnt about our mother's death. The sweet queen of Tyre was gone, and every purple fibre of my being rebelled against the darkness of war, the strong man's abuse, the murderous nature of the Assyrians. I had saved the youths of Tyre from a fate of slavery and savagery. Their skins would never be marked by a branding iron, their noses and ears would never be cut off. I had given them loving Cyprian wives; we had all chosen the sun and the moon and life itself, but o, Aeneas, you were death.

Those who remained in Tyre had seen their destiny collapse over them like a ruined temple. They were now either slaves or shadows in the coldness of the underworld.

Anna and I performed mother's obsequies that same day. The grave was empty but for our tears and the locks of hair we vouchsafed her for her journey. And thus I took her name, her Elisa next to my Dido. Thus I was to carry her memory not like a burden but as an identity, as you yourself carried your father and your Gods on your back. At least this way a part of her would live on in me and in our new city.

I soon ordered the construction of a sumptuous temple, dedicated to Juno, that Mediterranean Goddess, whom, next to Tanit, I envisioned would preside over Carthage.

A new era had begun for us, the exiles from Tyre that had found themselves beginning anew on the shores of Africa. The threat posed by the Assyrians meant nothing to us anymore. We were but a present waiting for a future in a land of nomad kings and men who loved the desert.

We lived in our new Carthage as we did in old Tyre. We loved the sea just as much, and it was the sea that brought to my shores the exhausted ships of yet another ruined people. We met melancholy men who, wretched in the present, saw glory in their futures and fires in their pasts.

Many moons had risen and fallen since the death of my mother. Anna and I shed our mourning robes like autumn leaves and we spent our days supervising the construction of the new temple. The friezes that bedecked the shrine of Melqart found their sculpted brethren in the female shrine of Juno.

The doors to this new temple also displayed scenes from the Trojan war: unhallowed tragedies by the sacred altars; the death of Priam at the hand and sword of rugged Pyrrhus, son of Achilles; the cries of Hecuba when she saw the young Greek make malicious sport in mincing with his sword her husband's limbs; the ravished cries of Cassandra, who still held on to prayer as though that could save her and a statue of Athena as though she would care… as if any of this could stop warlike rape of Ajax, son of Oileus; but no, the victorious vessels of the Greeks, laden with slaves and sorrow, sailed for home.

We took these foreign tragedies for our own. These stories, made famous through sea and land were our private woes. In them were the pain for our lost city, for the countless dead cut down by the Assyrian powers, and most of all, in them was the past, and all we had forsaken for the future's sake.

I was watching how, under the care of an artist, one of the friezes was bestowed with gradual life, when I was informed that a foreign embassy sought to converse with me.

I decided to meet them in the audience hall. I sat on a throne decorated with the skin of a panther black as night, and waited for these ambassadors. Three men soon entered the room. They were three Trojan warriors, as I could see by their warlike helms and the swords that hung by their sides. Their tattered clothes betrayed a long time spent at sea. Their general appearance inspired pity, and yet their deportment bespoke a great dignity.

I thought they must be princes, even as I mused on the fact that we had used scenes from the war of Troy to decorate our temple. Now these pictures were no such thing, they had left their frames and gained the quickness of the living. The men approached and kneeled before me, as survivors of unspoken calamities.

'O gracious Queen,' said the eldest of them, 'my name is Ilioneus, and these my companions are Serestus and Antaeus. Tempest-tossed we have arrived in your shores and we beseech your hospitality.

'We are neither pirates nor thieves; we do not pretend to ravage your land and ravish your women or drive your cattle into our bellied vessels. We are the sons of a tragedy named Troy, that same city that withstood a ten-year siege only to burn to ash. Our king is the noble Aeneas and we fear he is lost at sea. We have looked for him in the isles next to your coasts but all has been in vain.

'We humbly beseech you to allow us a short sojourn in your lands. We will sleep under the heavens if we must. Our king may lie forlorn on some forgotten shore, besieged by famine or thirst or some strange ague, and we shall not allow his body to go without burial, even if his life is gone by the time we find him. We also request that you allow us leave to stay until we are strong enough to sail for golden Hesperia, as the Gods have promised that land will be our home.'

'Noble guests, I thank the Gods for having brought you to Carthage. Your sufferings and stories are sacred to us; you may read your own lives on the friezes that bedeck our temples; the very doors of this hall teem with your tragedies and the images of heavenly Juno. There you will find as well, the story of my mother Elisa, who died in the heart of Tyre just as Priam died in the heart of Troy, taking the heart of Tyre and Priam took the heart of Troy.

'I am acquainted with the lineage of your king. Aeneas, son of Anchises and a Goddess, he who was begotten on the banks of the river Simoeis in the kingdom of Phrygia.

'I was but a child when Prince Teucer, a fugitive at the time, implored my father's help to arrive at Sidon. Those were Tyre's golden days; today it lies in ruins, and yet its glory lives on, as that of Troy does, in our memory and ourselves.'

Serestus stepped forward. He was a man of two score years, with nimble limbs and greying locks of hair.

'O Queen, your words reveal that hospitality is the second name of Carthage. Our twin cities, Tyre and Troy have shared the same shreds of a ruinous destiny, but the former will rekindle its glory anew behind your new-born walls. As for us, we have been ordered by the most mighty Gods to found a new city.

The prophecies say it will be eternal in its future, even if at present we find nothing but disaster–'

'–that shall be turned into good fortune. Carthage opens its doors to you and your noble brethren. If you so wish, we shall help you repair your ships and provide victuals for the journey to Hesperia; however, you are welcome to remain within our walls and society.'

Antaeus, the third of the noble company, now spoke. He was a man with a maritime smile and fire in his eyes.

'Would that King Aeneas were here to hearken unto the most noble of all queens!'

I was about to thank him for such a courtesy when Anna caught my eye. She was pointing towards the main door, through which two newcomers were now arriving. My heart started beating more strongly; it was a pain in my chest I couldn't get under control. Two men advanced towards me and I saw an expression of joy light upon the visages of my guests.

It is you, I thought when I saw one of the two newcomers. There was no mistaking your grey eyes, brown locks, and the memory of wind and loss that was engraved into the bronze of your face.

'Your wish has been granted, Antaeus,' you said. 'The Gods have driven Achates and me to the throne of this most illustrious queen, whom I can divine even now has some divinity in her.'

The Trojans embraced and you could see in their bearing the happiness of those who find loved ones after a period of absence. I myself experienced no lesser delight; I felt that I was about to cry, and yet

I managed to rule over my passion and retain the decorum that behoved my office.

'Aeneas and Achates, I bid you welcome to Carthage. It was given me by an African king and now it is yours as well. The very doors of it show that it was your destiny to come here.'

I could not believe what I had just said. But it hadn't been I who said it, but another voice. It had seized control of my tongue. It was a will that had usurped my heart; it was an injunction made by the Gods themselves, and its commandment bore the name of Love. But its second name is pain, Aeneas.

XI

You sent to your ships for your son, Ascanius. When the little one entered the palace, he carried with him a gold-embroidered robe, a saffron-coloured veil that whilom belonged to Helen herself; Ascanius also bore the sceptre of sovereign sway that ruled over Ilion, a golden crown, and a necklace of the clearest pearls I had ever seen, which yourself fastened around my neck before everyone.

In that moment my very bones started burning. I cried at night and yearned every morning for another day next to you. Then came days of revelry and banquets. We wanted no bard for the Trojan prince himself narrated the fall of storied Ilion to his Phoenician audience.

Many times your voice drowned in your tears. You spoke of glory and catastrophe, of death and hope, a hope that burned even as Ilion did. In your speech, we saw the smoking pillars of high-towered Troy, and we lived the fall of Tyre; we burnt in the Assyrian sulphur even as you bled in your words.

But in your destiny that wound was staunched: You were called the pious prince, a name given to you because of your love for the Gods and your people. And loved the Gods, you were ordained by Divinity and the writings of the stars to rear proud Troy's head anew, this time for eternity.

'You ask to hear of my disgrace, Queen Dido, and, for you, I am willing to venture into the waters of this most morose memory; therein lies that Greek stratagem, pregnant with death: the horse of accursed wood begot by the mind of cunning Ulysses. We all took it as a gift to Athena, all of us except Laocoön. The priest, truth-inspired, told us to keep it without the walls. When he pronounced those leaden words, two serpents, as arrows shot from the cerulean depths transfixed his flesh and crushed his bones. So did he perish with his two sons.

'I do not know what we thought. Maybe that the Gods were punishing him for impiety. Fearing such a destiny, we dragged our own death into our city, as Achilles dragged the corpse of our prince through the burning plains of Troy. The ominous horse then stood in the open square, and the women danced and the men revelled around it.

'That night the monstrous birth totalled our city. The Greeks poured out of the beast of wood, and, bronze-handed, crushed our chests with their cruelty. Cries flooded the city. The children drowned in them. We were slaughtered like game, not men. The dead quarry towered over the walls of Ilium.

'My quarters lay far from the citadel, that was what saved me. I looked for my father Anchises, my wife

Creusa, my son, servants, friends, whomever I could find, and we all ran towards the shrine to Cybele that lies beyond the walls, in the sacred forest.

'The tyranny of age had rendered Anchises almost an invalid. I slung him over my shoulder, while Ascanius walked by my side and Creusa a few steps behind him. Greek bronze, though smoking with gore still glittered in the darkness. Their weapons seemed to glow brighter than the fires that even now burned to ash the sacred city of Priam.

'Distracted by the imminent danger of death, exhausted by the weight of my woe-struck and weary father, blinded by the unruly black of the night only combatted by the flames of my lost city, I lost my wife. I do not know when we left her behind. She was swallowed up by the darkness, and ravened by the war.

'I left my father and son at the shrine to Cybele to look for Creusa. Several Trojans had run towards that beacon of divinity to escape the horror the Greeks had sowed on our city.

'I retraced my steps trying to make my way through the darkness. I yelled at the top of my voice, I yawped at the wind, howled the very letters of her name like a wolf. I did find her, or rather her shadow. In a dark street, her ghost greeted me with new horrors. She seemed greater than herself, more beautiful and further away than she ever had been.

'"Aeneas, my dear husband, stop looking for me, and start looking for your destiny. Jupiter did not wish me to accompany you outside Troy. Hark unto the message that The Everlasting has tasked me to deliver.

There is a land to the west by name of Hesperia. You shall travel thither, to the fields nourished by trenchant Tiber, and you shall found an eternal city. Forget Creusa, and be joyful that she shall not be a slave in some Greek palace. Goodbye, Aeneas, my husband, and keep Ascanius safe in both our loves."

'Thrice I tried to embrace her shadow, and thrice I failed. Those claimed by the darkness have no life or touch. Now, Queen Dido, noble youth, allow me to hold my peace, for memories live when they are uttered, and wage new wars that have already been lost.'

Aeneas sank into the pain of his past. I sat still on my throne and silence coiled around us like a fantastic serpent. The shadow of his wife had revealed his destiny to him, and I thought of how Sychaeus had done the same for me. In both our cases, a shadow had plotted out the escape route, the safe haven, and the future, but also this meant that we had no choice, no will but theirs. We owe our lives to the dead; they have left us, but we cannot ever desert them.

XII

And yet, if my will was not my own, it was less so my late husband's. Tanit had wounded me with her moonlight beams. I could feel myself bleeding. Tanit, or Aphrodite, or Venus (what mattered the name or language?) had shot me with a painful, terrible, silent and sweet shaft, and its name was Aeneas. I languished in life while I languished after you. Meanwhile, my duties as a queen and founder of a new city began to flicker, and soon my wick was all out and I was left in darkness except for the flame that burned inside of me.

I told you you could stay in Carthage while your ships were being repaired; one afternoon, driven to it by an incomprehensible start of my will, by an incomprehensible star above my will, I beseeched you to make my city yours.

Carthage could be yours, Carthage could have been yours.

Tyre and Troy would be joined like the serpents in the Caduceus. You could rename it if you so wished;

we could bring the assailed ashes of Priam and place them under a tumulus facing the sea.

***

Aeneas did not leap on the idea with any enthusiasm. But neither did he try to hasten the repairs his ships sorely needed to sail for his promised Hesperia. While in Carthage, he spent his days helping my men rear up temples and houses, plot the streets of the city, and teach the trade of war to the youths. All of this led me to believe that he wanted to stay in Carthage, that he wanted to stay with me. But it was nothing more than the foolish hope of a mad queen. My world was shattered into a hundred thousand shards because my heart itself was shattered, and yet I loved him with every piece of it.

Anna tried to keep my spirits up and sought to convince me that my feelings for him were guiltless. Sychaeus had died a long time ago, she would say, and she went as far as to say that Aeneas loved me back. I listened to her words as thirst itself thirsts after water.

The echoes of our conversations whispered themselves into my ear all day. He loves me? Are you sure? You love me? Are you sure?

Anna told me that she had seen how you looked at me.

'But I must confess he has never uttered a word about it to me,' she said. 'He is a melancholy man. Does he still miss his wife? We must consider how loving he is to his son. He won't let him out of his sight. But he loves you, of that I'm sure. Do you love him?'

'Yes and no. I am still true to the memory of Sychaeus. But it's like there is someone else inside of me, or something, that from the very depths of myself makes me love him. I feel like I haven't rested in years. He has taken my peace of mind, and all the pieces of my heart, and my plans and future. I cannot do anything anymore. I can't think, or decide, or command. The world screams his name into my ear; whenever I pour libation to the Gods, it is his face I see and not that of piety. The Gods do not understand it, they cannot understand how it is when they ensconce us in their wills and throw us onto this earth to war and love, to burn in or stifle our fires, to found new cities or to flee from them holding onto their statues.'

Aeneas. Aeneas. Aeneas… Your name followed me around, or maybe it was I who made it come out of the clouds and the earth. From within me it sprung out like the branches of a tree trying to reach out to the stars. Day and night mixed all around me. Time itself was but a stare, and it looked at Aeneas.

One afternoon I asked you to accompany me to the top of Carthage's newly-built ramparts. I beseeched you to look into the heart of this fledgling city, and to imagine how its name would soar through the sky before long. I asked you to envisage its promises of glory, its proud imperial dyes, its very heart of gold. Do you even remember?

You chose not to speak as that melancholy gaze caressed the body of my city. I could see the amber of the twilight reflected in your eyes, and I understood that you spoke in silence, with yourself and essence, with your dreams and past.

I, on the other hand, did not hold my peace. That something or someone inside of me, maybe inexorable Love itself, put these words upon my lips:

'Aeneas, all these horizons you see, all of this hope, is stretched at your feet. This city born through Tyrian pains under my command was yours even as you set foot upon these Libyan shores. I give it to you right now, under the sunlit judgement of Melqart.'

But I even wonder now if I knew I was not just speaking about my city.

'Aeneas,' I continued, 'my strength is no match to resist the pressure the Berbers put on Carthage and me. Some of them have expressed their wish to marry me, but I have remained loyal to the memory of my late husband. However, you and I can rule over Carthage together, as not so long ago I shared Tyre with the black memory of my brother.'

'Your words, Queen Dido, are like a breeze that may yet turn into a storm. I want nothing but to stay here with you, to rest from the toils of war and to change the sweat of blood for the sweat under the sun of tilling the land and building your temples. I want to see Ascanius grow and teach him the paths of virtue: to always tell the truth, to sail the fields, and plough the main.

'My men, likewise, wish to stay here. They only want to find a quiet place where they can bewail the past and water the fields of the present with their tears. Maybe one day they will harvest a new life.

'But at night, Dido, the shadow of my father haunts me. He reminds me what the Eternal has ordained. I have to build a new city on the fields of Hesperia, in a place called Italia.'

'Dreams often lie, Aeneas. Not all dreams come from Jove, some come from us and our fears and desires.'

'That thought has crossed my mind as well. It is the reason I haven't left for Hesperia yet. A battle rages on the fields of my being as we speak. And your beauty fights as Aphrodite fought alongside the Trojans in the ten-year war. You speak of suitor kings and a fire burns my soul. Black jealousy takes over me, unaccountable feelings, for you are Queen Dido and I am a fugitive; for you rule over the imperial dyes of Carthage and I have but my sea-ragged tunics and caprices.'

'Say no more, Aeneas, for you lie to yourself and me. You are a king amongst men, and the son of a Goddess. Forgive my forwardness and decide your destiny yourself, in complete freedom from my feelings and the injunctions of Heaven. Tomorrow, we shall hold a hunting expedition in the nearby forests. We shall hunt a ferocious boar or a lion, and shall offer a sacrifice to the Gods to grant us a reality for every one of our dreams.'

As we descended from the ramparts, I saw some silhouettes walking in the distance. I felt a hole in my heart, for it was none other than Jarbas, who casted his eyes through the curves of our city.

XIII

At the break of dawn everything was ready for the hunting expedition. I was the last to arrive at the meeting point. Sleep had not come easily to me that night and Aurora did not awake me as I had thought she would.

My horse awaited me, bedecked with the same colours that I wore. The brown and amber charger neighed and reared up in impatience, even as the hounds barked and savoured the air for the scent of their prey. Ascanius looked like twelve years of desire, astraddle a white palfrey that I myself had given him. The Trojan nobles looked forward to the expedition with a broad smile and, in front of the whole company, Aeneas distinguished himself with his usual dignified attire. His cloak was held in place by a golden broach with the image of a doe wounded by the shaft of a hunter.

Aeneas fell by my side and Ascanius let go of the reins that held back his youthful mettle.

Soon we found ourselves in the middle of the glades, following behind the hounds, their mouths watering after the glimmer of a scent.

Suddenly, the clouds came together in a conventicle of clamours, the sky went black and rain and hail poured down from the Heavens. The hunting party was scattered, each of us searched for a hovel or a cave to ward off the intemperance of the skies and immortal Jove's dread thunders.

Ascanius followed the Tyrian youths, while the Trojan company ran off in the opposite direction. Aeneas and I, however, made our way into some hidden cave. Inside, we calmed down the frightened horses and shivered off our clothes, heavy with hailstones.

We realised that we were alone, we did, you and I, and as if the will of Nature was within us, we both voiced and listened to the whispers of our destiny. I felt a heaviness lie upon me like lead; you must have felt it too, for you sought to lift that weight off me.

'Ascanius wanted to hunt a lion, but what he will catch is a cold.'

'He is used to the unkindness of the skies,' I said.

'He is yet but a boy,' you replied as you placed your hands on my shoulders and transfixed my soul with your grey eyes.

'Aeneas,' I whispered.

The storm grew in its harmony. A savage music made itself heard throughout the cave. The primeval smells of the earth climbed towards the sky and the Trojan prince and I fell in an embrace on the floor. Hymen and Tanit or Venus poured their amphoras of rich perfumes on us; the forest around us exhaled its rich resinous fragrances and Jove himself illuminated the sky for us. Through our love, the terror of his clamours turned into a light spectacle for our desire.

My hands caressed his neck and the tenuous spiral of his locks; his hands were on my waist and our breathing was like a veil worn on a marble statue. We were surrounded by ourselves and those winged thoughts of light and dark in my mind and his, our desires and obligations, obligation and desire, the best of all goods, the spring of woes unnumbered, love in grey eyes. Most of all, in that instant that has forgotten time itself, we were free from all those ghosts that haunted us, from the dead we had left behind.

**

We met the other members of our party under the smile of a grandiloquent sun. You and I rode together, continuing the silence of last day's twilight. Ascanius ran towards your wrapped up in an animal skin that someone had thrown on him. He looked at me anxiously. Young as he was, he could tell that his father belonged to him less than ever now. The other Trojans made their ways towards their houses and I to my rooms to dry my clothes out and smooth out the wrinkles in my thoughts.

When you stepped out of the cave I could sense you were overcome by inscrutable melancholy.

I am Queen Dido, not a green girl sighing after a man in the temple of Astarte, and so, I was resolved to hold a solemn supper next evening, and, before Tyrians and Trojans, to announce the coming nuptials of Dido and Aeneas.

XIV

The first person to arrive had not been invited at all, and yet King Jarbas walked through the doors escorted by two Gaetili warriors. I felt the very ground shake beneath my feet, but I was able to regain my composure soon enough. I was not alone anymore, Aeneas and his men would protect Carthage from the hostility of Libya.

'Greetings to you, King Jarbas.'

'I feel much offended that you did not think to inform me of the guests that have arrived in our land.'

'Our land? They have not trespassed on your territory, noble king. They have kept themselves well within the boundaries of this city and so they live in Carthage. I beg your pardon, King Jarbas, but I must speak candidly: as the queen of Carthage I do not have to justify myself to you or to anybody else.'

'I do not ask you to. I merely want to meet Aeneas.'

'You know his name.'

'His fame stretches far and wide. Now I want to see the dog that stole my queen from me.'

A fierce silence followed his words and seemed to cover the whole world.

It was a deep silence that he himself shattered.

'To kill him, of course.'

In that moment, you entered the room. Did it ever occur to you that someone else could want me? Walking by your side were Serestus, and Antaeus. Upon entering the room, you breathed the hostility in the air, and after identifying the Berber source of it, like a man tried in the trade of war, you put on his guard.

The African king gave you a look of death. I could feel Kenfas staring at me, as though he expected me to summon the guards. But I knew that Jarbas would not dare to attack you, not in the palace, at any rate. Surely enough, after a few seconds, Jarbas and his retinue exited the hall.

It was a solemn supper. The Phoenician youths and our Trojan guests made for a pleasant combination, lying as they did atop the sumptuous rugs that decorated the floors of the palace. When the krater was full and we had poured libation to the Gods, my lips caressed the brim of the same cup you had drunk from. You and I, forever, we joined hands and souls and announced our connubial union to an audience that cheerful celebrated the newfound alliance between Troy and Carthage.

Jopas, a bard of long hair, entrancing speech and eyes made dark by the most mighty Gods, rose from his seat and plucked his zither. He sang of love, of Alcestis and Admetus, that king for whom a valiant queen once descended into the depths of the world to give herself up in his stead... all so that her love might live again. Would you ever do that for me? No, no, if we meet in Hades, I will not go with you. I love you much to much to suffer your love again.

Jopas sang of the stars in the sky and the toils upon the earth; of the birth of a glorious *urbs* that, as we stared into each other's eyes, we thought would be ours forever.

XV

How mistaken I was! How blind; blind and stupid,
deprived of my feet and hands and senses by the cruel
bounds of Love… Love… tasked by the mighty Gods,
Love sculpted my ruin out of the marble desire of my
destiny. I just wanted to please you, you basilisk.

***

I wanted to cater to his every wish, to throw
innumerable gifts and pleasures on him. But,
industrious as he was, every morning he left me to
supervise construction work in the city: the houses,
temples, docks, his own ships… His men still worked
at them, but their purpose was not anymore to carry
them to Hesperia, but to aggrandise the glory of
Carthage. Aeneas wanted to stay; he wanted to make
of this new city a Troy with a new name.

Every night I would embrace him and beg him
never to leave me. He would feign anger and reply
'how could I ever abandon my wife?' I would laugh
and go to sleep asking Tanit to give my love an heir.

But one of those nights he awoke from a nightmare, sweating fear through all of the pores on his skin.

'Where is he? Where is he?' he screamed.

'Where is… who?' I asked him, feeling crushed by the blackest presages of future sorrow.

'My father! He was just here, sitting on the edge of the bed. He spoke to me and told me… O, Gods!'

His fingers tore at his hair as though they were hooks of metal. It was as if he wanted to rip out his own skull. I wanted to embrace him, to comfort him as one would a child, but he pulled away from me, hurting my very soul.

'My father says you have led me astray from the path the Gods had chosen for me. Their wrath is upon me.'

'It was but a dream, Aeneas. From what path have I led you astray? You have found your home in Carthage; a realisation to your dreams. This is your city. I am your wife.'

Haunted by the ghost of his father, Aeneas looked at me scornfully. I did not try to comfort him anymore. That was the first night he spent away from my arms since our wedding ceremony. In the following weeks, similar nights made me weaker and followed in wake to his black dream.

The next day I was told that a strange woman sought an audience with me.

I had never seen her before, neither in the palace or the city. She was of a swarthy complexion and I could not guess at her age, for the number of years she had inside her was simply indecipherable, as though written in some strange language. She said that her name was Lamia, and professed to know the arts and mysteries of what lies beyond our mortal spheres.

'What is your speciality?' I asked, driven to a forbidden knowledge by a vague curiosity or perhaps an impossible hope.

'Love,' she answered, staring deep into my eyes with her cat-like pupils.

'I have no need of your services. I already have a husband.'

'Yes, Prince Aeneas.'

We were public figures; there was every reason for her to know his name. And yet I could not but feel that she possessed the blind insight of futurity.

'Queen Dido, the stars have whispered to me that the Gods wish to ruin you. Aeneas is to leave Carthage. What their injunctions are, how they are to be accomplished, when or why, I do not know. Flesh as we are, we can only hear noise, mist, and uncertainty.

'We are the prisoners of the present and all its mirages. The Gods know that we are tangled enough as it is in our own webs of ambition, and yet it is so. They see and live eternity. For them, there is no yesterday or tomorrow, only a today that we could never understand. In it, they are eternal, while we are shadows of nothingness.'

'I do not understand. You're rambling.'

'Listen to me, Queen Dido. You have chosen wrongly. Some time ago, the Gods spoke to you through Jarbas. They allowed you a glimpse of the paths of life and death; you have chosen Aeneas, and with him the pyre. Its fire will drown all tears. Nobody will weep, not even that man who unloves you even as you love him, not even the ashes of Sychaeus or the Gods that see it all.'

A silence settled above me: it was as though the wings of a raven had eclipsed the sun. I was to die? Aeneas was to leave me? Who was this old hag?

'And yet,' she continued in the whisper of a snake, 'there is still time. Banish the Trojan. Cover your brow with ash and beseech Jarbas for an audience. He will know what to do.'

XVI

I went to see Jarbas that same afternoon, driven to it by Aeneas' last nightmare and rejection. The guards outside his tent showed me to him with what I thought betrayed a weary negligence on their part. The villains! They thought they would gape at the humiliation of Queen Dido…

Inside the tent, Jarbas was conducting a sacrifice. I wondered what kind of Gods he worshiped. As a denizen of the desert, he should have payed homage to the stars above us all, but inside the tent I saw an altar to high-ruling Jove, he of the triangular stele. Jarbas pretended not to see me.

'Hear me, o father of the Gods! Jupiter *Omnipotens*! Wherefore have you forsaken me, when I have always been the first to do you homage? You favour the Troadian impostor? That rascal who has broken his vows to heaven and has climbed to an adulterous bed! I myself asked for the queen's hand and she rejected me to keep her ash-bound honour. Change your allegiance and your will, you Everlasting, and awe us with your justice!'

Far in the distance a thunderbolt burnt the sky white. Like the lightning, a cold shiver ran down my back. Jarbas did not look at me for several minutes after his invocation was finished. When he did turn his head, I saw something like despair in his eyes and I at last understood the immense sorrow with which he loved me.

'I listened to your prayer, o king. And the answer made you by the God you addressed. Presages direful swarm me, and I have not forgotten that dream wherein you saw me die dressed in flames.'

'I do not recall that dream, Queen Dido. But answer me this, why did you not invite me to your fateful wedding? The fortunes of our states are tied indissolubly.'

'I was afraid you'd find it insulting. You did ask for my hand, or have you forgotten that as well?'

In that moment, Jarbas knocked over the altar in a fit of violence. Jupiter's triangular stele fell to the floor like a shattered star. I thought that a terrible catastrophe was afoot even then. He stood shifting his gaze between the ruined God and me. Whatever it was I stirred within him overcame his piety and fear.

He took me by the shoulders and tried to kiss me. Like thunder follows lightning, the whispers of Lamia went through my mind. Maybe it was not too late and maybe I could save myself from Aeneas' scorn. Maybe I could escape death itself in the embrace of this Berber king. But it was the face of the Trojan prince that I saw inching its way towards me. I saw the grey eyes of that prayer I voiced so many years ago, when I was but a mere girl. The Love, the impossible Love I bore the Trojan was now strangling me like the embrace of a serpent.

I rejected Jarbas.

'Let destiny run its curse,' I said.

'May the Gods take pity on you, Queen Dido,' he said as he turned his back on me.

XVII

When I got back to the city I donned a grey robe and decided to spy on Aeneas. I looked for him at the main construction site, but met not him nor success. It wasn't until I walked to the docks that I saw him from afar. He was not in the company of his men but a long way off, speaking with a strange young man I had never seen before.

I turned my sights to his companion. He was a youth of extraordinary beauty and an aristocratic air. No noble newcomers had arrived in Carthage that day that I knew of, and I made a point of being informed of the new arrivals at my city, which of late had been quite substantial. Carthage grew in fame and its glory spread through the waters of the Mediterranean like sunshine.

A hand lighted on my shoulder and I could not help but flinch. My soul quaked when I recognised Lamia.

'That youth with whom your husband now converses is a God. He was sent by Jove, to grant the prayer of Jarbas, his favourite amongst all mortals.

Even now he's telling Aeneas that he must leave these shores, that in your bosom lies his perdition, that he is letting down the memory of his father, and that if he does not hie away from here, he shall lose the eternal glories of Hesperia.'

'You lie, you witch,' I said weakly. 'Jarbas has hired you to hurt my soul. He wants to take over my city. But you won't get away with it. Prince Aeneas is here to save me from that. I love him. Against the will of Jarbas, against the injunctions of the most mighty Gods, and their messenger phantoms, I love him. He will not forsake me. He has given me his sword to prove his faith to me. We are Dido and Aeneas, we shall be so, and will be together for all eternity.'

Each word I uttered made me less sure of what I spoke; each syllable drove me deeper into my personally-brewed hell. Lamia, meanwhile walked away from me. But before leaving me for good she pronounced these words:

'You will come to me in three days. I will be by your side to cut that silver thread, Queen Dido.'

I turned around to look at Aeneas and his mysterious companion, but the youth had disappeared. My husband was now surrounded by his men. They seemed ill at ease, and, looking over their shoulders, they made their way towards their ships.

What was happening? Aeneas walked towards the palace with a heavy pace. I followed him from behind and could mark how he stopped before the threshold of those quarters we had shared for the short lifetime of an immolated infant.

I loved you there, I loved you more than the Gods allow mortals to love; past myself, past love itself. And you did not go in. You turned on your heels, you turned towards the oars of your ships instead of my arms. That's when I knew I was forlorn. That's when I knew you would leave me.

The coward did not even have the courage to tell me so.

Night came over my soul and the caverns of my being echoed with the howling of the solitary wolf of death.

XVIII

I had lost sight of the Gods. I had lost sight of the stars over Carthage; most of all, I had lost sight of myself and my great purpose. What could I do but call Anna to find something of mine in the likeness of her face?

But written on her visage I could only see how like a stranger I looked to her. Then the mirror itself scorned what was reflected in it: hollow cheeks and vagrant eyes. Was that me? Can somebody tell me who I am? That creature, that dislocated creature, was it Queen Dido, or just her shadow in a mirror?

'Anna *soror*,' said I, 'have you heard the rumours? The Trojans are about to leave us?'

'Are they? What, and leave Aeneas behind?'

'Prince Aeneas himself is the reason of their leaving.'

'You're going with them, then?'

She did not once for a second think Aeneas did not love me. I could hold my tears no longer. They broke out of me like a tumultuous river. I embraced my sister and cried and cried, breaking that promise I had spoken to my father so many lifetimes ago.

'He is leaving me. He has been taken away from me by his ghosts and Gods. He has to be true to ancient oracles and phantom prophecies. Anna, o, Anna, any excuse would have worked for him, as it does to those who have stopped loving, who perhaps never loved. He did not even dare to look upon my face to say goodbye. Go to him. Ask him to have mercy on me, ask him to stay; tell him he's leaving me defenceless against the African kings… They will soon suspect my weakness and storm our walls.'

'Your sister need not speak to me, here I am. Use your own voice.'

If the silence was terrible, his words were like the stare of Medusa. I could not move from my chair; my tears were petrified on me, and my shame was naked, for him and all to see.

'Leave us, Anna. I'll speak to him alone.'

'What I am come to say can be heard by her.'

I felt as though an asp had bitten me. He did not want to be alone with me. He would never hold me or kiss me again. My whole world was over.

'I must take my leave and sail for Hesperia. I have incurred the Gods' wrath by tarrying here too long, by marrying you. Cloud-compelling Jove sent a messenger to me; the shadow of my father visits me nightly. You do not know how terrible those fatal visions are. Every particular hair on my body stands on end, a direful panic takes hold over me. Were these enemies men, were they mortal, I would not be afeared. I would disobey the injunctions of Heaven, were they not of Heaven. I would do it for you, for your city. But these are Gods, Dido. My father screams from beyond this world and I hear his cries. I must not abide in Carthage any longer. I thank you for your gifts and your friendship–'

'My friendship?' I asked in disbelief? 'The most savage of beasts is of a milder nature than you, Aeneas. Friendship? How can you say that? I love you. We have lain together in a connubial embrace. I gave you my city and its destiny, and myself and my destiny. I gave you all!'

'And in good time you gave it. But the shepherds of the people are not like other men. To us duty comes before desire; the future before the present. Whether you want to accept it or not, the Gods have spoken.'

'The Gods are wrong!' I bellowed barbarically. 'But you're right. You must go. Go! Now. Get out! Your sole presence here is insulting. Accursed be the day in which you came to my shores. I would pluck out those eyes that saw you and took your semblance to my very heart if I couldn't use them right now to see you leave.'

He said no more. He left the palace and never came through my doors again.

XIX

I sought solace in the sights of temples, in religion, in the sighs of memories and in the dead ash of a once-husband, and it was all for nothing.

I turned to Juno first. I had raised the tallest temple in the known world to her, and to her I went, blind, deaf and dumb with pain, to find some cure for this sorrow that stole the air from my lungs and the blood from my veins.

I walked solitary over the marble floor as I saw the oil lamps blink, as though they wished to close their fires and not see my pathetic figure. I walked towards the altars where incense burns forever; there, I poured libation with my tears, and then with my spirits. But almost immediately, to my horror, the wine I poured as a queen and a priestess broke down into fetid smells, so foul they seemed to desecrate the holy air in the temple.

I would never tell that to anyone, not even to Anna. Carthage wouldn't know that its queen was accursed, that her hours were black as Hades, that her hands corrupted everything they touched... Was there a way to go back? To those days without you, to Sychaeus, or his sepulchre, those days when I was the crystal star of Phoenicia, the godlike Dido Elisa?

I dragged myself towards the temple I had risen in honour of Sychaeus. I turned the afternoon into a black night, and felt the pain it bore on each one of its hours.

The finest marble, the softest fleece, the most aromatic garlands bedecked the walls of the temple. The amiable soul of my late husband rested enthroned in the majesty of these walls.

I really thought that he would understand, that he would comfort me; never did I think that it was I who had abandoned him, broken my faith, that I had betrayed his memory when I was taken into the whirlpool of a terrible love inspired by a vengeful God that fateful day when the Trojan vessel arrived in my shores.

The moment I stepped into the temple, all of the lamps went out. A gelid wind shook the tapestries on the walls. The night owl shrieked a horrible damnation and I could hear in its uproar the hidden voice of Sychaeus, calling to me, crying, cursing, showing to me all his pain and all his death, his soul with its throat split open as his body was by my brother. But this new wound had not been caused by a dagger wielded by a misguided Phoenician but by Queen Dido of Carthage.

XX

I went back to my own palace, wrapped in the fire veil of my despair. It burnt me black, my bones singed inside me, my pupils hurt whenever one of a myriad images of you passed through them. Those who saw me turned their heads in horror, but I did not care, for I walked towards death.

I tried to fall asleep, I sought to steal a few seconds of rest from that very same bed in which, unhappy as I am! you and I had lain together. I had dreams terrible in which I wandered solitary through sea and land trying to carve a nation for the Tyrian people out of the rock of this rough world. In the middle of my dreams I heard your voice, beseeching me to leave you alone; you said that my love was an obstacle, that I was detestable to you and the Gods, and to your father and Ascanius.

I woke up exhausted but resolved.

Lamia was waiting for me inside the palace the next day. She had arrived in the early hours of the morning, as if summoned by my dreams. There she stood, with an indecipherable look on her face and her cat-like pupils; her voice was like that of a snake. And I felt triple Hecate was behind her ageless form.

But I was finally calm. I called Anna, who entered my chambers with a timid step and regarded the sorceress with alarm.

'Do not fear her, sister. I have called upon her to help me regain Aeneas' love, or to help me get rid of him for good.'

The two of them helped me build a pyre. We went to your chambers and retrieved your arms, your cloak, your sandal, and that simulacrum of you that I had commanded be sculpted so that I could behold your features when you were not with me.

'With this we will destroy the memories of him,' said the sorceress in rusty words. With that gnarly and dry voice she summoned the Gods of the eternal night, Hecate of triple form, Erebus and Chaos.

Inside my mind, two winds fought for supremacy: the love of life and my need for death; but a third wind was missing, the love of my life.

I thought of Jarbas and his eyes of night and his arms around my body. Let the garlands burn, let memories be scorched to ashes. Let passion burn in its own fires, until it is reduced to smoke and soot and nothingness.

I, Dido Elisa of Carthage, daughter of Belus, widow to Sychaeus, mother of Nobody... atop this pyre I myself have reared, took the sword of that cruel man that left me, and fell on it. I felt the happiness of its edge, the compassion of the blade as it sliced my life open, my skin, my lungs, the engines of pain that had besieged my heart, and then I collapsed into the fire.

I failed to die instantly; I saw Anna cry, I saw Lamia tear at her hair, I saw the Gods confused at a death that was not supposed to happen. And I saw silver-footed Iris come down from the ether to the earth, and Lamia come up to me with a youthful visage and a pair of silver shears with which she cut one of the hairs on my head.

My soul let go and my life itself was dragged by the very winds that right then drove you away from Carthage.

XXI

We lived, Aeneas, Aeneas, Aeneas... We lived the golden days that the Gods save for themselves, days in which I woke up amidst your embrace, in which your warlike shield and sword hung undeeded over our bed; days in which you kissed me goodbye to supervise the construction of a temple or a house.

Ascanius explored my palace, the boy had a Tyrian tutor and learnt the letters of Cadmus. He learnt about rivers and peoples, their lineages and the wisdom of the stars. I prayed to Tanit for a son by you, a son with your blood, your locks of hair, and your deportment. I am glad I did not teach him tyranny.

At night, we opened the coffers of our desires and our eyes wept happiness over the shadows; the shadows of Sychaeus and Creusa likewise wept tears of smoke; not too far away, in a Gaetili tent, a Berber king cried as he plotted your death and made sacrifices to Jove asking us to be punished.

But none of this mattered to me when you were by my side. Back then, I could not ever cast enough looks at you. I could not stop staring at your grey eyes, could not stop getting lost in them and feeling that I was melting into you, into your transparent gaze, into a veil or a breeze that is as a wave of the sea. You made me less of me. Who am I any more? Sometimes I wonder whom I'm addressing, whether you or myself or if there is any difference at all.

And then the day came when I learnt you no longer worked on my buildings. The houses went unheeded by you, the towers were left unprotected, for you repaired to your ships and left me for Hesperia.

At first, I did not believe it, Aeneas, Aeneas, Aeneas... because that same night you had kindled the heavens with your star-like kisses, because you had whispered my name in the shores to my seas.

And yet I ran, and I saw you ordering your men, plotting maritime courses on your maps. Then you told me that one of your Gods and the colossal shadow of a lost father commanded you to leave a plague-stricken city. You had to leave my city as though it were a den of lepers; you had to sail for Hesperia where you would find a pure *urbs* and a better wife.

It made me mad, Aeneas. I yelled, I spat at you, I insulted you, I called you ungrateful, I wanted to bash my skull against the walls of Carthage, I wanted to flay the day and have the night rule forevermore. I wanted no more of it, no more of your ships, no more of my city.

I am claimed by Hades now. I have deceived everyone. You, my people, my sister. I made a pyre of scented woods, surrounded by garlands. At the very top of it, I placed your warlike shield and sword, your simulacrum, that same piece I had made to gaze upon you when you were away, to kiss you when no kisses where to be had, to worship your parts and features.

I told everyone it was a spell to expel the ill luck you and your Trojans brought to my shores. I instructed an African sorceress to invoke the Triple Goddess, and I, with my tunic undone, my hair knotted and frayed, with a sandal slipping off, put an end to the misery known by those who love more than the Gods permit.

Goodbye, Aeneas. Even now I can hear the rumours of your departure, the hallooing of your men, the voices of your sails and the inscrutable language of the waves. I laugh when you think you can decipher the language of the Gods. You can't understand their writing, you can't distinguish between the noise of eternity and their voices.

Goodbye, Aeneas.

I merely go before you. You are the son of a Goddess, but just as mortal as I am. I was happy in your embrace and in the infinite lakes of your grey eyes.

To other lakes will I travel now; my soul shall cross in darkness the desire it still has of your name. And when you finally come here, when death claims you, my shadow, still in love with you, will meet yours again.

To end this weary life, just know that I, through eternity, through dust and ash and the glimmers of light, perfumes, winds, and, footprints, will always be Dido, Queen of Carthage.

ARS

FVTVRA

Made in the USA
Middletown, DE
25 March 2025